EXAMINED AT THE HUCOW PRISON

Steamy Milking Story

Leandra Camilli

ISBN: 9798837709425
Imprint: Independently published

1st edition

Cover design by: Leandra Camilli

CONTENTS

CHAPTER 1

My friend nudged me on the shoulder slightly, showing me that he was finally crossing the courtyard. We were seated on one of the benches positioned around the basketball field, some of the inmates already playing. The sun was hot and the sunlight was so intense that it made me block it with my hand, trying to see the doctor as well as I could.

He was holding a suitcase, his gait hurried and determined. I had no idea where he was going, but I sure as hell hoped he was heading in my direction.

The only problem was… I knew he wasn't, and my friend was a jerk for showing me that Bernard finally left his office today. He was one of the doctors that worked at the prison, and he was the only man that stirred something different in me.

Even though he was several feet away from me, I already felt a hint of heat between my legs. Without even thinking about it, I moved my hand down, finding my mound, though I didn't do anything to it more than scratching it slightly with my finger, and even then, I still had my clothes on.

I wasn't supposed to be wearing clothes right now, but I still was. No one was going to change my mind about that.

As always, Bernard was crossing the courtyard without giving anyone as much as a glance. He didn't have to, after all. The ring on his finger showed me that I would never have a chance with him no matter how much I tried. That was why I was looking at my friend with judging eyes, showing my discontentment.

What the hell was she thinking, making me remember that he

was the only man in this prison that I would never have anything with?

"You know that nothing is going to happen between me and Bernard," I grumbled, and she waved her hand, showing me she didn't believe that.

"I don't think that's exactly true."

In the meantime, my eyes couldn't stop scrutinizing every part of Bernard's body. The best thing about him was that he was incredibly, lust-inducingly tall. I could just imagine myself in his arms, his chin resting on my head, feeling the warmth of his body as his hands explored every part of me.

Even though he wore his doctor uniform, it wasn't enough to fully hide his well-built physique.

He was unbelievably athletic, his hair always looking sharp, was short, his face had a thick stubble, and his eyes were always showing how certain he was about what he wanted.

They were brown, deep eyes. The kind of eyes of a man who knew who he was and that nothing could ever surprise him. I supposed that was one of the reasons why I wanted to feel him inside of me, to be sliding my mouth over his cock, enjoying every part of it, and then trying to figure out how thick he was.

"Look, I think he's going to the gym," Brenda pointed out, and I noticed she was indeed right about that. I didn't think he was going to the gym – was he in a hurry or something like that? He never went there unless he was going to work out, in which case I was going to take a peek.

Nothing surprising about that. After all, I wasn't the only one that was going to watch him as he worked out, something that made me feel a hint of jealousy in me.

"We should go there before everyone else steals our spots," I suggested and Brenda leered, hurrying over after me seconds later. She was bigger than me, her boobs jiggling as she followed along.

It wasn't long until we were at our spots. We were in front of everyone that had come here to take a long, careful peek at the doctor. But it was also going to be much more than that, wasn't it?

We were going to be spying on the doctor as he pumped weight and worked his hard muscles. Ahhh… the moment I was waiting for was already happening. Bernard was removing his clothes, showing his perfect, delicious body.

I dissected it from top to bottom with my hungry eyes, wondering how it was possible a body could be as perfect as his. I couldn't help but wonder what it would be like to move my fingers over his muscles, feeling every part of them, every curve, and pretty much everything else, including the sweat on his skin.

Even from where I was standing, I was feeling as though he was right in front of me. After all, the temperature of my body was beginning to increase. Brenda glanced at me again, leering.

I knew what was going on in her mind. Even though we were mates, when it came to the doctor, we were competitive.

But time was passing and we were both beginning to realize that we could never – and would never – be able to steal the doctor's attention. It made me think about his wife and what she looked like. Was she as curvy as I was? What was the color of her hair? What did she like to eat for dinner?

So many questions and they were all flooding my mind right now.

Bernard made his way to one of the machines. I didn't know what it was called. He grabbed the bar, sat on the seat, flexed his muscles, and then pulled down the bar, his muscles rippling and looking more taught.

Everyone that was spying on the doctor drew in a short breath, and I could feel the heat radiating from their pussies.

I felt the same way, but in the meantime, as my eyes cherished what I was seeing, the only thing I wanted was to plan. To create a mechanism so that I could finally steal his heart, to become his plaything so that he could impregnate me.

Why was I saying that? The reason was simple. When hucows were in heat, we needed to be knocked up, and it was always a no-brainer. When we were pregnant, we could and would make more and better milk. I was an inmate and also a hucow, so I had already gotten through the initiation process.

Everything I wanted right now, though, was to finally have my first time with a man - something that didn't happen yet.

I did have my first time with Brenda, but it wasn't as good. It wasn't good enough, to be more precise about it.

I'd sucked off her pussy, enjoyed it, cherished it, and it was then I found out I was bisexual, but I wanted more and I wanted the real thing. I wanted a man like Bernard to finally pop my hymen.

Was it going to happen? I didn't know, but recent days were pretty hectic, and I was wondering if things were going to take a turn for the better for me.

CHAPTER 2

The doctor finished working out in the gym, turning around slowly as he ignored once again that we were all spying on him. I was certain he knew what we were doing, but he was deciding to ignore it for the time being. His abs shifted and flexed, the shadows following the movement, and it was as breathtaking as I thought.

Then, he tilted his head up, finding my eyes. For a moment, I thought I was only imagining things, his hand holding the cloth that he used to wipe the sweat off his forehead.

Did he just look at me, out of everyone hiding behind one of the walls? It was possible, but I didn't think it was likely. After I blinked, the first thought that came to my mind was that I probably only imagined it. I mean, it had to be, right?

Moments later, he went to the bathroom, where he was going to take a shower. Nobody dared go there with me, not even Brenda, so I was going to have to go there alone. I glanced at her, quirking up my right eyebrow. Just to make sure that she really wasn't coming along, I asked, "Not coming? Really? That's disappointing."

She waved her hand, showing me she didn't care about what I was planning on doing, even though that couldn't be the case.

"I don't think I want to take the risk."

I shook my head in disapproval. Without thinking twice about it, I whirled around, taking off after Bernard. I knew why I was the only one still chasing him. I was the only one dumb enough to do that, and also the only one who thought he had looked at me, even though that couldn't be the case. He was taken and was happily married to his wife, right?

A moment later, I was finally hiding behind a wall, controlling my breathing as much as I could. It was difficult to do that, though, especially when so many things were on the line right now. After all, if Bernard noticed that I was here, he could make it so they took me out of the prison, something that would destroy me.

My heart sped up, my head peeking to see what Bernard was doing. I heard him turn on the shower head, close the door of the shower box, and then step inside it.

I knew that what I was doing was wrong, but there was no stopping it anymore.

I moved my body so that I could better see what he was doing. One of the good things about this gym was how empty it always was. It was why I knew nobody was going to come. I had all the time in the world to do what I was, my hand moving down and finding my clit.

Without even thinking about it, I was already stripping off my clothes, my body so hot I thought I was going to explode. I took another step toward Bernard. The steam fogged the shower box, which meant I couldn't see him as perfectly as I wanted.

And knowing that he was naked, I knew I could steal a glance at his dick, finally figuring out something that was eating me from the inside out. How big was he?

Finding out the answer to that was almost a matter of honor.

Seconds later, I finally managed to achieve what I was looking for, but there was something different about that – he was turned to me, seeing me.

Shit! When did that happen? I thought he was actually going to be looking the other way. After all, when I first started to approach him, making sure that my footsteps were controlled and weighted, I thought I was doing it right.

But it appeared that I was mistaken about it. Either that or something outside of my control had just happened.

Then, he put his hand on the shower box's door, pulling it to the side and opening it. He wasn't just looking at me – he was glaring at me.

I didn't think he was going to be so pissed off that I was spying on him.

"I think I might know your name," he rumbled, making me realize his voice was deeper than I'd thought. I had heard it when he transformed me into the hucow I now was, but it was still surprising, making me feel shivers down my spine.

"What?" I squeaked, moving away from the doctor even though I knew it was a lost cause. Now that he knew I was here in the bathroom, with him, spying on him and still rubbing my clit as though I thought that was going to change anything, he was more than ready to inflict rounds of punishment on me.

"I said I know your name. I was there when you were changed," he rumbled and started to take steps toward me, and I tried to run away, but when he grabbed my hand, I knew that it was over.

And yet, something in me told me he was only going to keep on going with this as long as he thought I was willing.

CHAPTER 3

"How about we do this in the infirmary?" He asked, realizing that I was more than willing to withstand whatever punishment he had for me. His hand was hot as he continued gripping my hand. Then, he lifted me and put me on his shoulder, showing me how strong he was.

I could feel my skin on his wet skin, and it sent shivers of excitement in my body.

I never thought this would be happening. He was holding me on his shoulder as though I was nothing more than a toy. And the best thing about that? Bernard was already stepping outside the gym without putting his clothes on.

Everyone in the courtyard turned their heads to look at him, their eyes bulging as they realized what was happening. The first thing that was crossing their minds was how jealous they were feeling right now. After all, they never thought that Bernard, the hottest doctor in the prison, would ever have eyes for anyone, much less me.

Even Brenda was looking at us wide-eyed. As Bernard crossed in front of her, she asked me, "How the hell did you make this happen?"

But Bernard was too fast and I didn't have enough time to reply. In less than a couple of seconds, he was already taking me down several hallways before we reached the infirmary. He settled me on a raised bed, his eyes gazing at me as though he was wondering what he should do to me.

Glancing down, I realized I was finally having the moment I

most sought only a couple of minutes ago. I'd been wondering how thick and long he was, and now I could finally have the answer to that.

It was difficult to find the right numbers, though. He was probably 10 inches long, and who knew how thick.

Bernard noticed my reaction, stepping toward me as he put his fingers around his prick. "You like what you are seeing, don't you?" He asked, brushing his fingers on my forehead as though I was nothing more than something he could play with and abuse as much as he wanted.

Even though I knew that the last thing was something he could do, I knew he wasn't going to. He was imposing his dominance over me, but he was actually respectful as well. His hand was calloused and warm on my forehead, and I enjoyed it, feeling his fingers still brushing there, over and over as if he wasn't even thinking about ever stopping it, letting it continue for all of eternity.

I nodded. There was no point in keeping the truth hidden from him, and he knew that.

"Well, you are allowed to put your fingers around my prick," he announced, and I didn't know how to react. It was one thing to know that I could do it, and another to finally do it.

My hand was shaking, but I still lifted it. As I did that, I realized how futile my whole efforts before this were. Had I known before that he felt something for me, that he had eyes for me, then I would have been braver about this, letting him take me to the infirmary so that he could put me on this raised bed just like he did.

He moved his hand away from his cock and I finally had the opportunity to put my fingers around it. When I did that, the first thing I noticed was that I couldn't make my thumb touch my other fingers. It was the first time that happened, and I didn't know what to think about it.

Before this, I'd played with some cocks and they weren't anything like the one I was enjoying right now. His cock was even throbbing, which was one more thing that never happened before.

I started to stroke the skin slowly, up and down, and I didn't even know what I was doing. I could see his balls, imagine how heavy they were, and I just wanted to be playing with them, too. I guessed that the doctor had noticed that too about me, for he grabbed my hand and then moved it to his balls, and I was able to start playing with them, finally being sure about something I thought before – his balls were indeed heavy, and much more so than I'd thought.

"This is all happening the way I wanted it to happen, but there is something missing," he said, moving away from me until I wasn't with my hand on his prick anymore. When that happened, the first thought that crossed my mind was how unfair it was.

What was Bernard thinking, stepping away from me without as much as warning me? I didn't know, but the first thing I wanted to do now was to slap his face until he said he was sorry, and I knew that would never happen.

He walked to one of the cabinets in the infirmary, opened the door, and then picked up something from inside it. I didn't know what it was, but I didn't have to wonder about that for long. In less than a second, he turned around, showing me what it was. It was a hospital mask, and it indeed fitted the occasion.

"I'm a doctor, so I think I should look the part," he said, but I knew that what he did wasn't enough – at least not for him. Then, he did something I thought he wouldn't. He went to another cabinet, opened it, and then grabbed something else from inside it.

It was an apron. It was white and looked neat, and it fitted him perfectly. Even though he could dress more like a doctor, I knew he wasn't going to and the reason for that was at the tip of my tongue.

And I knew he could read my face as though it was an open book.

"I'm happy you are enjoying what your eyes are seeing, but I think that this is enough clothing for what we want to do," he said as he started to pad over to me. I took a deep breath in, realizing that this was indeed happening and that nothing could stop it.

"Are you ready to be examined, Gloria?"

CHAPTER 4

When he asked me that, the first thing I noticed was that someone was spying on us from the small window in the door. It took me a while to realize who it was, but when I did, my heart skipped a beat. I knew that she was feeling jealous about this, but I didn't think it was so severe.

It was Brenda and she was behaving as though she wanted to barge into the room, rip me off the raised bed, and then offer herself for Bernard. Even though I knew that was what she was thinking now more than anything, she was still going to keep her lips sealed. After all, she would never show me she was envious of something I achieved.

Bernard stopped where he was, making me wonder what he was thinking. Then, he showed me what that was. He looked over his shoulder, finding Brenda as she finally ducked as fast as she could even though it wasn't good enough. She wasn't fast enough and I was certain that Bernard noticed her.

"Looks like someone wants to join in on the fun. Do you think we should let her in?" Bernard hissed and the only thing I could do right now was to shake my head. It didn't matter how much I liked Brenda – she wasn't going to get in the way of me losing my virginity. I could just imagine his thick, throbbing prick breaching my pussy, destroying it, stretching it, and doing other things to it I didn't think possible.

Seeing that, Bernard chuckled and resumed coming toward me. He was across the other side of the raised bed, then he put his hands on my legs, moved them apart, and bent his body down slightly, putting himself so close to my pussy I could feel his breathing on it.

He looked up, his eyes twinkling in the darkness of the room. I didn't know what he was thinking, not even turning on the light so that he could better look at my begging mound. But I realized that wasn't important to him, for he soon started to explore my snatch with his fingers, moving them up and down slowly and gently, feeling every part of it, checking every section, and also instigating ripples of pleasure in my body.

It was difficult to control my feelings and what he was doing, tormenting me. The way his finger flicked up and down, sliding on my pussy, prying the lips, pulling them apart, and doing pretty much everything else he could think of were all more than enough to make me feel as though I was running out of oxygen.

Seconds later, my breathing sped up, my eyes rolled inside my head, and my body started to writhe and squirm, everything around me looking blurry. When I finally climbed down from my orgasmic high, I noticed that the doctor just finished playing with my snatch, using his finger as he did so.

He was looking up from between my legs, and I noticed that they were trembling slightly.

"That was amazing, Gloria. Do you want me to make that happen again?" He asked, making me realize he made me come just by teasing my cunt with his finger, making me feel ripples of pleasure in my body.

His eyes were glaring at me and I knew he wasn't going to drop his question until he got the answer he wanted. I supposed it was for that reason I could only nod. And I did that and as soon as I did, he leered. If there was something that Bernard was good at, other than his doctor skills, it was the way he smiled.

It was always so leery. It was like it was the only thing he could do when he felt he was on top.

In the meantime, I tried to shut my legs, but he was quick to stop that, putting his hands between them. "What do you think you're doing, Gloria?" He asked, sliding his hands up on my legs. "You can't change what's happening, and it's pointless anyway."

I felt my breathing stopping when he put his fingers next to my quivering and leaking mound again. He swiped his finger on it, catching some of my wetness. Then, he moved it toward his mouth, licking it clean. I knew he was going to do that, but it still came as a surprise.

He took a deep breath, closing his eyes as he tasted my wetness as much as he could. "Jesus, it's all good. Do you want to taste it too?"

I wasn't going to deny that the thought of doing that was tempting, but it was also weirdly disgusting.

In the meantime, I just noticed that I was lactating. Lines of milk were coming out of my nipples. They were engorged, big nipples, so different from what they were like before – when I wasn't a hucow.

Bernard noticed that, padding over to me slowly, putting his fingers on my right boob. He pressed them into it slightly, enjoying the moment.

"Ohhh, look at this thing," the doctor said, watching as lines of my milk spurted out in the air, hitting his face and his apron. I thought he was going to be annoyed by that, but he wasn't. He was still leering from behind his mask, and I knew he wanted to see more of that.

In the meantime, his cock dangled between his legs, inviting me to touch it. But was he going to allow me to do that again?

CHAPTER 5

I couldn't deny that my lips were dry, as was my throat. His cock was just so big and tempting. The more I thought about it and the more I looked at it, the more I wanted to touch it, to feel it, to do everything possible with it.

And the best thing about this moment? It was that he was leaking some pre-come from the slit in the cockhead.

But it appeared that Bernard was more concerned about something else. I felt his fingers moving around my right boob and I knew he wanted what was inside of it. He wanted more of it. He showed me that when he coated his finger with my milk, moving it up and toward his mouth, which he licked clean.

That was a lot, just like it was the first time he did something similar. Seeing that, I could feel some heat forming in my pussy, something that made me squirm slightly. I thought that it was just an involuntary movement he didn't notice, but when he put his hand on my leg and started to press on the skin with his fingers, I knew it was a lost cause.

He started to massage my mound with his thumbs, bending his body down so that his head was right behind my ear. "I know how much you want me to do that, how much you want me to take your virginity, but it's not going to happen right now. Your examination is still ongoing."

After he said that, he bent his body slightly further down, rubbing his lips around my nipple. If I thought that it couldn't look any more engorged and bigger than it was, I was wrong about it.

It was so big when it was in his mouth, milk still coming

out in hot, long spurts. He was enjoying that as much as he was cherishing the taste of my milk. In the meantime, I could feel my body trembling, his hands keeping me down as though he was afraid that I was going to roll off the raised bed. But that wasn't going to happen, especially when his intention was to keep me tied down to it as much as possible.

"You are so delicious, especially when you are so submissive," he said even though he was with his lips still sucking my milk, enjoying as much of it, and there was so much of it coming out that it was actually leaking from between his lips.

When he stopped sucking my milk and he pulled his head back up, his lips were smeared with my milk. He was still leering at me and looking at his face, then at his lips, and I couldn't help but wonder if he would be okay with kissing me right now. But if there was also something about Bernard he never told me, but which I knew was true, was that he wasn't the kind of man that kissed.

I knew that with so much certainty I was aware there was no point in even asking him about it.

That would only make me feel even more humiliated than I was. I always thought that I would never submit myself to any man, but that was what was happening at the moment. I was so submissive to him that I would let him do anything to me he wanted.

"There's still the other breast," he said, walking around the raised bed and putting himself until he was by my side. His eyes checked me again, from bottom to top, and then he put his hand on my left boob, pressing his fingers on it until my milk was coming out in hot, long spurts.

Some of it fell on my belly, and then he put his right hand on it, keeping his left hand pressing on my boob. Without giving me a warning, he bent his body down, enclosing his lips on my boob again. When he did that, I felt ripples of pleasure in my body, and then I closed my eyes, knowing that this was only the beginning.

Or maybe it was the end. After he sucked out more of my milk – as much as he could – he walked until he was across the other side of the raised bed again. He grabbed both of my legs and lifted them up, pulling me to him slightly and until my legs were over his shoulders, enjoying every moment of this as much as he could.

I could see his chest expanding and contracting as he breathed, his eyes checking every part of me as though he could see and read what I was thinking. In the meantime, it was like time had stopped around me, and my mound continued to tremble, waiting for him to pierce it.

"You know, I thought I was going to drag this out as much as I could, but I think that I don't want to do that anymore," he said, pulling me until his cock started to nudge my pussy, and then he pierced it without a fuss, going all the way inside of me after he also popped my hymen. The way he just did that, so simple and yet so efficient, was everything I thought it was going to be.

It was painful, his length stretching my cunt as much as he could, and then he started to roll his hips slowly before picking up the pace. I started to match him thrust for thrust, and then I came at the same time as he did, his sperm filling me, coating my walls, and I knew that I had just been knocked up. I could already imagine myself with his baby in my belly, and it was something that would bring me pleasure and a sense of pride.

I took a deep breath in and closed my eyes, knowing that I was going to fall asleep, but still doing nothing to stop that from happening.

EPILOGUE

renda was looking at me wide-eyed. She didn't believe what happened. She thought I would never get pregnant and much less that it would be none other than Bernard that was going to do it. But now, after stepping out of my bedroom, I was looking at her with a sense of pride in me. Nothing was better than proving to someone that they were wrong and that I was right.

I mean, I never thought that Bernard would even have eyes for me, but now it was different. I was nothing more than a toy he could play around with, but it was better.

The doctor was still married and lived his life as though nothing changed, but he always came here looking for me. His intentions? They were simple. He wanted to keep fucking me, to knock me up as many times as he could, even though that couldn't happen right now.

I was only a couple weeks pregnant, stepping out of the place where I was after they made sure everything was okay with me.

"I still can't believe that I'm a virgin and... here you are, looking so proud of the fact that you were knocked up," Brenda grumbled, going with me as I felt how difficult it was to walk when my body was so heavy. It wasn't just my ass and boobs that were oversized, but also my big belly. It was so big that I knew it was only going to get worse, and walking around was going to be so difficult. It was so much so that I was even sweating right now.

Then, when we were getting into the courtyard again, I noticed that Bernard was still in his office, bent over the desk as he worked on something. I didn't know what it was, but just seeing his face, his muscles, his body, his lips, and pretty much everything else about him, I wanted to go to his office right away.

Brenda knew that too, which was why she was leering at me. She patted me on the shoulder, pushing me forward slightly. I snapped my head back to her as I glared, wondering what the hell was even going on in her mind, doing something like that.

Was she trying to knock me down or something like that?

I didn't think much of it, just going over to the doctor's office, knocking on the door, even though it was open. He looked up from his desk, pushing his chair back and widening the gap between his legs.

He was without his mask, showing me how perfect his face was, his jawline, his nose, and even his intense eyes. The more I looked at it, the more I wanted to kiss him, but that was something he said he would never do with me. He was probably afraid that his wife would find out about it, in which case hell would break loose.

"Do you want to suck me off right now, princess?" He asked, standing up. He appeared to be feeling lazy right now, and I thought it was for that reason he sat back down on his chair a moment later.

He didn't just lower his pants, but also his pair of boxer briefs. His cock was finally free – just like it was so many times before when we were together – and it was as tempting as ever.

Getting on my knees was difficult, but I managed to, and then I was with my face right in front of his junk. I licked my lips, finding it difficult to contain how much arousal my body was feeling. It was like it was burning my skin, and even moving my hand was difficult, even though my arm was a part of me that wasn't heavy yet.

"You can do whatever you want to it, princess. This time, I'm sure that you're going to make me come in record time," he said and I knew that it was much more than words. He wanted me to know that I could make this the best blowjob he would ever get.

Without even thinking about it twice, I put my lips on his

cockhead and then my fingers on the base of his manhood, enjoying the feeling of it trembling underneath.

Bernard tilted his head back, moaning as he said, "Gosh, you are so good at this," he murmured, and I started to suck him off slowly and nicely, moving my head up and down.

I covered the entire length of the stick, and I could feel my mouth watering, enjoying how thick and meaty he was.

In the meantime, I was already leaking some milk from my nipples, and the doctor was so naughty that he couldn't help but reach out with his hand, applying pressure with his fingers, enjoying my boobs as much as he could.

"I'm never going to get tired of how smooth and soft your udders are," he murmured. In the meantime, I couldn't stop enjoying every moment of this, moving my head up and down, working his stick for as long as I could and I knew he was going to come in my mouth.

When he was doing that, I knew how much pleasure I would be feeling. It would be so much of it my body would start to tremble, I would start to get sweaty, and everything would be bliss.

Minutes later, it was finally happening. He was coming into my mouth and it was the most exhilarating, breathtaking thing that ever happened to me. It wasn't as good as the first time we had sex, though. It was lust-inducing, and I knew that I was going to climax without even doing anything special.

And I did, my eyes rolling inside my head. It was difficult for me, thinking about everything that transpired before this moment, and I knew how much I wanted to be with the doctor for as long as possible.

It wasn't going to be much different than it was right now, though. I was going to continue being his plaything and he wasn't going to get a divorce.

Still, it was a dream come true.

The End

Looking for the other books in the series? Find them here:

1. Condemned to the Hucow Prison
2. Shared at the Hucow Prison
3. Passed Around at the Hucow Prison
4. Chained Up at the Hucow Prison

Thank you for reading this story, and leave your review. Your feedback helps me immensely!

TEASER: CHAINED UP AT THE HUCOW PRISON

Steamy Milking Story

"There was someone I knew that was in your position," the lawyer said, looking at me with concerned eyes, even though, checking out his face, I knew that he was feeling no pity for me.

It was like he was trying to convince me to do something, but I had no idea what that was.

I was in his office and he was sitting across the desk, looking at me as he reclined in his chair. He was absolutely stunning. One of the most handsome men I had seen in my life.

One of the things I first noticed about him when I stepped inside his office was that he was so much taller than me. I could see that my eyes were level with his nipples, which was something that didn't happen often.

Most of the men I knew weren't that tall, where I lived. I could just imagine myself in his arms, feeling the heat of his body, the beating of his heart, his fingers dancing on my skin, feeling it, and then his hot lips crashing down on mine.

Just thinking about that happening was already hardening my nipples, which was, in turn, making me blush. Dammit! I had no idea what was going on with me, but this was concerning on all levels.

Charles was most likely looking at me and wondering what I was thinking. I looked so innocent, too, even though I was anything but. I couldn't help myself. My hands were clasped between my thighs and I was trying to make myself as small as possible, even though that wasn't working well.

After all, if there was something that people always told me I was, it was that I was curvy and busty. And yes, I pretty much was. Those were some of the few things about me I was proud of and that I always rubbed in the faces of the people I didn't like.

Usually, those were my enemies. Girls from my former high school class that thought I was less than them. But then I proved I wasn't, and now here I was, talking to my lawyer, who was most likely going to give me two options - either go to a normal prison or the Hucow Prison, and thinking about the latter... I couldn't help but feel extreme levels of anxiety.

I just never thought that this would happen. I thought that nobody would find out about what I did to my enemies. Those bitches... I hated them so much I just wanted to see them dead.

That wasn't what I did, though. It was something much less drastic.

"Ms. Cisneros?" Charles asked, his head behind his hands and his elbows on the desk, looking at me as though he was thinking about asking another question, but he was going to weigh his words better this time. After all, this was more difficult for him than it was for me. "You need to think about your choices and what you can do."

And with that said, I perked my head up. "Take me to a normal prison. I don't think I want to go to the Hucow Prison."

And having said that, he took a deep breath and then stood up and went around the desk. My heart started to beat faster than normal, and I could feel sweat coming out of the pores of my skin. He was going to go behind me, wasn't he?

It was an idiotic question. I knew he was going to do that, thus it wasn't surprising when I felt him putting his hands on my shoulders. The audacity of this man! And yet, something about the way that his fingers were pressing against my skin sent cracks of electricity through my body.

My pussy was beginning to get wet and I couldn't do anything about that. I was just hoping that his nose wasn't perceptive enough. If that wasn't the case, then for sure he was going to notice the smell of my arousal.

"I think I can change your mind about that," he murmured behind me and even though his face was far from my head, I still felt his hot breath swirling around my neck, sending ripples of arousal down my spine.

"What do you mean? I just don't want to be subjected to a place where they are going to milk me and change me so much that I would be unrecognizable."

I could hear him sniffing and I knew he was smelling my arousal. Realizing that made me feel even more concerned than I was, and I started to rub my legs together, doing everything in my power to contain my increasing arousal.

But it was all pointless. I was getting hornier and hornier by the second, and Charles was using that to his advantage.

"If you decide to go to a common prison, your sentence won't be lowered, you won't be able to see anyone you want, you won't get any money for anything you do there, and you will also live there for so long that you will come out of there completely unrecognizable. I know it's up to you, but I think that the best option for you is pretty clear. Spend a couple of years in the Hucow Prison, get milked a couple times, and then come out of there looking like a heroine that doesn't owe the world anything."

I wasn't going to deny that it was tempting, but I couldn't even think about that properly when he was with his nose almost rubbing on the back of my neck.

Then, he moved away and sat back down in his chair. He clasped his hands together on the desk and then gazed at me with questioning eyes.

"So, have I managed to change your mind?" He asked and I finally had enough space and time to think about it more clearly.

Then, I closed my eyes, thought about it a little more, and decided to choose my words carefully so that I didn't make a huge mistake.

"All right, I'm changing my mind and I'm going to the Hucow Prison, but I hope that I'm not making a mistake."

He opened a wicked smile.

"You aren't."

SIMILAR BOOKS

SERIES - FAVORITE HUCOWS

1. First Time in the Barn

2. First Time in the Pen

3. First Time in the Shed

4. First Time in the Tractor

5. First Time on the Haystack

SERIES - FERTILE ONLY

1. Bumping the Teacher

2. Bumping the Midwife

3. Bumping the Farmhand

4. Bumping the Sinner

ABOUT THE AUTHOR

Leandra Camilli's obsession? Writing dirty, steamy stories that make her readers drool. She loves her Alpha males, hucows, sissies, and futas. If you're looking for those kinds of books, look no further.

With a cup of coffee on her table and warm socks on, she writes almost every day. Leandra Camilli has featured in several top 100 categories in the store, and she publishes weekly.

www.ingramcontent.com/pod-product-compliance
Lightning Source LLC
Chambersburg PA
CBHW052137150726
48002CB00006B/2650